# Bridesmaids Club

# Fairytale Wedding Wish

Posy Diamond

# With special thanks to Linda Chapman

ORCHARD BOOKS

First published in Great Britain in 2020 by The Watts Publishing Group

1 3 5 7 9 10 8 6 4 2

A CIP catalogue record for this book
is available from the British Library.

ISBN 978 1 40836 097 2

Printed and bound in Great Britain by Clays Ltd, Elcograf S.p.A

The paper and board used in this book are made from wood from responsible sources.

Orchard Books
An imprint of
Hachette Children's Group
Part of The Watts Publishing Group Limited
Carmelite House
50 Victoria Embankment
London EC4Y 0DZ

An Hachette UK Company
www.hachette.co.uk
www.hachettechildrens.co.uk

# Contents

## Chapter One

Cora finished brushing Star's silky mane and hugged him, breathing in the sweet smell of pony. "On Christmas Day, I'm going to decorate your mane with tinsel and give you a big feed with lots of carrots and apples," she told him. Outside, in the frosty stable yard, she

heard a car horn beep for the second time. Reluctantly, she put the brush away in her grooming box. Star nudged her with his nose, looking for treats.

Cora rummaged in her pockets and found a couple of pony cubes. They were a bit fluffy, but Star didn't mind. He snaffled them from her open palm, the whiskers on his muzzle tickling her skin. Cora kissed him.

*BEEP . . . BEEP!*

The car horn sounded even more impatient now. Cora sighed. "I guess I'm going to have to go before Horrible Helena explodes." She pulled a face. "I wish she *would* explode and disappear,

Star. She's so annoying. I can't believe she's going to be my step-mum by Christmas." Star snorted softly.

*BEEP . . . BEEP . . . BEEP!*

Cora knew she had put off going home for as long as she could. She gave Star a last hug, checked he had enough water and left the stable. She walked slowly over to where the shiny, black car was waiting for her, its engine running. Her dad was sitting in the front passenger seat, Helena was in the driver's seat and behind her sat her five-year-old daughter, Mollie May. Mollie May was chattering to Helena and Dad, her hair a halo of blonde curls around her head.

Cora opened the door and got into the back beside Mollie May, her boots and socks shedding straw on to the pristine car mat.

"What took you so long? Didn't you hear the horn?" asked Dad.

"Yeah, I heard it," Cora said.

Her dad turned to look at her over his shoulder. For a moment, she thought he would tell her off, but he just sighed and turned back to the front. "Right, well, let's get going."

"Can we have the music on, Mummy?" asked Mollie May as Helena started to drive away. "Pleeeease!" As usual, Mollie May had a princess dress on. She had a whole wardrobe of them, along with a shelf of tiaras and sparkly shoes. Today, she was dressed as Sleeping Beauty in a frothy, pink outfit.

"Of course, sweetie," said Helena, turning the sound system on. The music from *Frozen* filled the car and Mollie May started to warble along.

Cora groaned. "Do we have to listen to this again? Can't we listen to the radio?"

"But this is my favourite!" said Mollie May, her mouth turning pouty as she started to frown.

"Don't I know it," muttered Cara.

"I want *Frozen*!" said Mollie May mutinously, glaring at Cora.

"We can have your choice of music in the car tomorrow, Cora," said Helena. "And Mollie May's today. OK?"

Cora scowled. Why did Mollie May always get first choice? Helena and Dad spoilt her rotten. Mollie May started to sing again.

"Dad!" Cora protested, leaning forwards. "We always do whatever Mollie May wants. It's not fair!"

"That's not true," said Dad. "Stop being so grumpy and join in. You used to like this song."

"Yeah, when I was a baby!" said Cora.

"I'm not a baby!" Mollie May protested. "I'm a big girl!"

Cora slumped down in her seat as her dad joined in with the song and encouraged Mollie May to sing with him too. He didn't get it. He really didn't understand how much she hated living with Horrible Helena and Mollie May. Just because he loved them didn't mean she did, too. When they'd moved in a few months ago, he'd said she might enjoy having a sibling. But Cora liked being an only child. She didn't want a little sister, particularly not an annoying one like Mollie May who just wanted to play princesses. And she didn't want a step-mum either, especially not a glamorous, fashion-obsessed one like Horrible

Helena, who was now joining in with the singing and throwing soppy glances at Dad. *Yuck!*

Cora pulled out her phone to see if there were any texts from Emily, Shanti and Sophie. She and Emily had been best friends ever since they had started at Crosshills Primary School but they had only really got to know Shanti and Sophie, from the other Year Six class, a few months ago. At the beginning of the school year, the four of them had discovered they were all going to be bridesmaids and had formed the Bridesmaids Club, with the aim of helping each other be the best possible bridesmaids. They agreed that being a bridesmaid wasn't just about wearing a pretty dress and carrying flowers; bridesmaids were supposed to help the bride and make sure the wedding ran smoothly.

Sophie had been a bridesmaid at her mum and dad's wedding. They'd planned to have a wedding abroad but then Sophie's dad lost his job and it had looked like the wedding would be called off. The Bridesmaids Club had come to the rescue and organised an amazing wedding on the beach at home instead.

Then Shanti had been her sister Rekha's bridesmaid and had been

desperate to find the perfect wedding gift to give her. The Bridesmaids Club had helped her solve that problem too, by performing a special dance for the bride.

The next wedding was going to be Cora's dad's. It was taking place right before Christmas in just a few weeks' time. Cora knew her friends thought she should feel more excited about it – it was going to take place in a real-life castle, just like in a fairytale. *It's exactly like being in a fairytale,* Cora thought crossly. *I've got a wicked stepmother and an annoying stepsister. I just wish I had a fairy godmother too, one who could grant my wish – of cancelling the wedding!*

There were no messages from her friends when she checked her phone, but of course Sophie would still be at her swimming training and Shanti and Emily would only just have finished their dance class. *I'll text them later*, Cora thought as Helena parked the car in the driveway of their house.

They lived in a large modern house with big windows and a semi-circular driveway in front of it. Cora and her dad had moved there two years ago – a year and a half after her mum had died of cancer. He'd wanted a fresh start, but Cora had wanted to stay in their old terraced house that was full of memories of her mum. That was the problem with being a kid – you didn't get a say in where you lived, or who you lived with. You just had to put up with whatever the adults decided.

Cora got out of the car and marched to the front door. It had a huge holly wreath on it with big white bows. Cora much preferred the pine wreaths her mum used to make each year. They had dried orange slices in the oven and then Cora and her mum would tie them on with red ribbon. Just looking at the new, shop-bought wreath made her heart clench.

While her dad brushed the mud and

straw out of the car, Helena, who was wearing a tight, dark pink dress, teetered round in her high heels to Mollie May's door. She undid the seat belt and helped her daughter out of her car seat. Mollie May started dancing round on the front lawn, making her long dress swirl out. "Look at me, Mummy! I'm a princess!"

Helena laughed. "You'll be even more like a princess tomorrow when we go to the wedding dress shop and you and Cora try on bridesmaid dresses!"

Cora's heart sank. She preferred jeans and hoodies and she was dreading shopping for bridesmaid dresses. But Mollie May squealed in excitement.

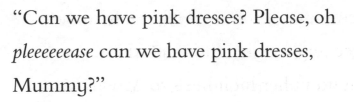

"Can we have pink dresses? Please, oh *pleeeeeease* can we have pink dresses, Mummy?"

"Oh, no, not pink!" Cora burst out.

Dad was beside her, opening the front door. "What's wrong with pink?"

"I hate pink!" Cora exclaimed, all of her unhappiness spilling out. "People who wear pink look stupid!"

Helena and Mollie May looked at each other. They were both wearing pink. Cora saw the hurt in Helena's eyes. Mollie May's face fell.

"Cora, that was rude," Dad said.

He was right, Cora knew that, but too many emotions were swirling

through her – frustration, guilt, anger.
She couldn't bring herself to say sorry.
Instead, she ran upstairs to her room.

When she got there, she flung herself
down on her double bed with Max, her
cuddly toy horse. The blue walls of her
room were covered with pony posters
and clothes were scattered over her floor.
The door to her en-suite bathroom was
open and that wasn't any tidier – there
were towels on the floor and a jumble of
shampoo and shower gel bottles on the
shelf.

She heard the sound of footsteps
coming up to her bedroom and then
there was a knock on her door. "Cora?"

Dad said softly, looking in.

"What?" Cora muttered into Max's neck. Her strawberry blonde hair had fallen across her face and she didn't look up.

Dad came into her room and sat on the edge of her bed. He gently touched her shoulder. "Are you OK? Are you finding all the wedding stuff hard because of Mum?"

*Yes!* Cora wanted to say. Words swirled in her head: *it's like we're forgetting her and I don't want to forget her, not ever. If Mum can't be with us, I want it to be just the two of us, like it was before Helena and Mollie May came along . . .*

She wanted to say those things, but looking into Dad's concerned blue eyes, she couldn't get the words out. She knew it would hurt him and she didn't want to do that. She loved him and she knew he loved her.

"Cora?" he said softly. "Tell me what's going on, sweetheart."

She shook her head. "It's . . . it's nothing. I'm . . ." She swallowed. "I'm sorry I said that stuff about pink being stupid."

Dad's forehead creased. "When you first met Helena, you said you liked her. But ever since she and Mollie May moved in, you've been so moody."

Cora tried to put it into words. "I guess Helena's a bit like a meringue."

"A meringue?" echoed Dad, puzzled.

"Yeah. It's OK when you have a little bit, but you get sick of it when you have it every day."

"Oh, Cora-Flora," Dad said, using the name he used to call her when she was little. "Everything's going to be OK, I promise. I know it's going to take time to adjust, but I bet you'll soon find yourself enjoying our new family."

Cora turned her face into Max's soft back. *Like that's going to happen,* she thought.

"It really would mean a lot to me

if you could put up with all the girly bridesmaid stuff," Dad went on. "Will you go shopping for dresses tomorrow with Helena and Mollie May – for me?"

Cora heaved a sigh. "OK," she said.

He kissed her forehead. "Thank you. Now, I'd better go and make supper. Come down when you're ready."

Cora nodded and watched him leave.

As soon as the door closed behind him, she pulled her phone out of her pocket and texted the rest of the Bridesmaids Club – Emily, Shanti and Sophie.

Emergency! Have to go bridesmaids dress shopping tomorrow with the Wicked Stepmother! HELP!!!!

## Chapter Two

"I really don't want to go dress shopping this afternoon!" Cora groaned as she sat with her Bridesmaids Club friends at breaktime. They were perched on a wall at the edge of the playground, wearing warm winter coats and gloves.

"Trying on bridesmaid dresses is fun,"

said Sophie. "I loved it when I went with my mum and Aunty Allie."

"But I'll be with Horrible Helena and Mollie May so it won't be fun at all," sighed Cora. She shuddered. "Can you think of a way I can get out of it?"

Shanti twirled one of her long dark plaits around her fingers. "How about saying you're going to come to a new dance class with Emily and me tonight?" she suggested.

"If I do that, I bet Mollie May will want to go too and they'll find out I'm lying," Cora pointed out.

"OK," said Emily. "Well, how about saying you have to buy some art supplies for a school project."

"No good. I've got loads of art supplies already. Besides, Helena loves any type of shopping," said Cora.

"What about Star?" suggested Sophie. "Can't you use him as an excuse? Say you've got to look after him tonight."

"I guess I could," Cora said slowly, considering it. "Dad pays for him to be mucked out on school days, but I could tell Helena that Alix, who usually does it, isn't able to look after Star today."

"You're going to have to go and get a bridesmaid dress at some point though," Shanti pointed out.

"Unless I can persuade Helena to buy mine online," said Cora. It was worth a try!

As Cora came out of her classroom at the end of school, Helena was waiting in the playground wearing a glamorous navy blue dress and heels. She ran a fashion business and had come straight from work. Her blonde hair was carefully curled and she looked happy. *Probably because we're going clothes shopping,* Cora thought.

Mollie May ran out from the Infants building and hugged her mum. Helena hugged her back, then caught sight of Cora and waved. "Time to go dress shopping with my lovely bridesmaids!" she called, coming over with Mollie May. "Are you excited?"

"Actually, there's a bit of a problem," said Cora quickly. "I had a text and

Alix can't do Star today. I'm going to have to go to the stables instead of shopping." She'd actually sent Alix a text at lunchtime saying not to do Star today.

Helena's smile faded. "Oh."

"But, Mummy, I want to try on pretty dresses!" whined Mollie May.

"Can't you ask someone else to look after him today, Cora?" said Helena.

"Nope, sorry," said Cora. "I can't leave Star without food and with a dirty bed."

"No, of course, you can't," agreed Helena. She bent down to Mollie May, who was starting to pout. "OK, here's what we'll do, Molsy – we'll take Cora to the stables. You and I can wait in the

car while she sees to Star and then we can all go shopping afterwards. How about that?"

Cora's heart sank. Helena usually did everything she could to avoid going to the stables. She was pretty sure Helena hated horses. "It'll take quite a while to muck him out," she said. "Maybe you two should go and look at dresses on your own."

"No, I want both my bridesmaids there," said Helena. "We'll wait for you."

Mollie May nodded. "I can help you, Cora. I like horsies!"

"I think you'd better stay in the car with me, sweetie," said Helena.

Mollie May's mouth set in a stubborn line. "But I want to help Cora!"

"All right, all right," Helena said, giving in before Mollie May had a tantrum. "You can help Cora and then we can go to the wedding dress shop afterwards."

Cora groaned inside. That wasn't what she had planned at all!

They stopped at home to get changed. Mollie May seemed really excited about going to the stables. "I love ponies. I want to learn to ride," she said, taking Cora's hand as Helena locked the house.

"But Mummy says I'm not old enough yet."

"Yes, you are," said Cora. "My mum started teaching me when I was only three." She felt her heart twist in her chest. Her mum had loved horses. Cora had a photograph of herself, aged four, sitting on her first pony – a little Shetland – next to her mum on her big horse, Bella.

"Can I ride Star today, Cora?" Mollie May asked.

"No," said Cora. "He's too big for you." She had to admit, she felt a bit surprised at Mollie May's eagerness.

As they were about to leave, Helena

got a work phone call. "I'd better take this," she told the girls. Cora sat in the car feeling bored as she listened to Helena's side of the conversation. She zoned out as Helena talked about fashion stuff.

"I know! I saw them this afternoon," said Helena. "I thought they were going to be lilac, not bright purple. They're absolutely hideous!" At last, she ended the call. "Sorry about that," she told the girls. "I had a consignment of shoes come in today and they're not what I was expecting at all. I don't know what I'm going to do with them!"

Helena drove them to the stables.

When Cora got out of the car and breathed in the familiar smells, she felt a rush of happiness. The stables were her favourite place in the world because they reminded her of her mum. She helped Mollie May out of her car seat. "Come on, Mummy!" squealed Mollie May excitedly.

Helena opened her door and peered out, her face wary. Annabeth, the yard owner, was leading Duke, a large grey horse, back from one of the fields. He passed near to the car, his hooves clopping heavily on the tarmac. "I think I'll just stay here," Helena said hastily, shrinking back into the car. "I've got a few more phone calls to make. You two go ahead. But please look after Mollie May, Cora. She doesn't understand how dangerous horses can be. Don't let her out of your sight."

"I won't," Cora said. "But you must do what I say, Mollie May. You can't yell or squeal or jump," she warned the little girl. "Horses get scared by loud noises or sudden movement. OK?"

Mollie May nodded, her eyes wide and solemn.

Cora showed her around the muddy yard. Mollie May wanted to see everything! She giggled as Star whinnied at Cora and gasped in delight as Star gently took a treat from her hand. After tying Star up outside his stable, they made up his feeds together and filled his bucket with fresh water.

"I like it here!" said Mollie May happily as Cora showed her how to stuff clean hay into a haynet for Star. "Can I come again?"

To Cora's surprise, it had actually been fun showing Mollie May around the stables. The younger girl hadn't had a tantrum or whined once. "Yes, you can," she said, nodding. "And I'll teach you how to groom Star next time if you like."

"Yes please!" breathed Mollie May.

"Girls?" Helena had ventured into the

barn and was picking her way round the puddles and straw, trying not to get her shoes muddy. "Are you going to be much longer?" she asked, her eyes flickering around as she reached the stable door. "If we don't get to the shop soon, it'll be shut."

"Well, we still have to muck out," said Cora. She saw Helena look at the dirty straw bed and wrinkle her nose. "If you help us we'll finish a lot more quickly," she added mischievously. "Can you please get me a wheelbarrow and pitchfork? They're just over there," she said, pointing to the wall.

Helena bit her lip. "OK." She headed

over to the mucking-out equipment.
"Um, Cora . . . Star's in the way."

"Just ask him to move," said Cora.
"Touch his side and say 'over' and he'll
move."

Helena took a tiny step towards Star.

He whickered hopefully, thinking she
might have a treat.

Helena leapt back. "Um . . . on second
thoughts, maybe I'll leave you to it
and we'll go dress shopping tomorrow
instead." Giving Star a very wide berth,
she half-walked, half-ran back to the car
park.

Cora raised her eyebrows. What a
surprise – Helena didn't want to get her

fancy clothes all mucky!

She showed Mollie May how to muck
out and when they were done, they put
Star away in his nice, clean stable. Mollie
May gave him a hug as he munched on
his hay. "Right, we'd better go back to
your mum," said Cora, heading over to
where the car was parked.

Helena was leaning against the car,
talking on the phone. Her voice floated
over to Cora. "Yes, well, I'm going to get
the money and then I'll get out fast," she
said, laughing.

Cora felt as if she'd just had a bucket
of ice tipped over her head. Was Helena
talking about marrying Dad? When her

mum had been alive they hadn't had much money, but her dad's software company had been bought by a much bigger business and now he was wealthy. Was that the reason Helena was marrying him?

Looking up, Helena spotted Cora and Mollie May. "I've got to go," she said quickly into the phone. "I'll call you later. Bye."

"Who was that?" Cora said, her mouth dry.

"Just work," Helena said.

Mollie May ran over to her mum. Her cheeks were pink from the cold air, her hair was full of hay, her jeans covered in

horse hair, but she was beaming. "I love the stables!" she said to her mum. "Cora said I can help groom Star next time I come here."

"In you get," said Helena, quickly lifting her into her car seat.

Cora got into the back beside her. Helena started the engine and put the car heater on to warm them up. Mollie May chattered about the horses all the way home. Cora didn't say anything. The words she'd heard Helena saying were echoing in her head: *I'm going to get out fast.* It sounded like she didn't intend to stay married for very long. *Poor Dad,* thought Cora. *It would break his heart.*

She stared at the back of her stepmother-to-be's head. She had to do something to protect her dad from getting hurt – but what?

## Chapter Three

"Isn't this fun?" said Helena the next afternoon as she, Mollie May and Cora walked through the bustling shopping precinct towards *Wedding Belles*, a wedding dress shop. A group of carol singers were singing by a huge Christmas tree and all the shops had

twinkling displays in their windows.
"What could be better than a fun
Saturday out with my bridesmaids?"

Mollie May skipped beside her, holding
on to her hand. "Trying on pretty
dresses!" she said happily.

Cora didn't say anything. Her eyes
were scanning the precinct. *Yes! There they
were!* Her heart lifted as Emily, Shanti
and Sophie waved and came hurrying
towards them.

"Hi!" they chorused.

"What are you doing here, girls?" said
Helena in surprise.

"I hope you don't mind, but Cora
asked us to come along and look at

dresses," said Sophie politely.

"We all love weddings," added Emily.

Helena looked taken aback for a moment but then she smiled. "Shopping

for bridesmaid dresses *is* fun, isn't it? By all means, come with us. You might even see some dresses you like, too. You're all coming to the wedding, aren't you?"

"Yes, we got our invitations, thank you," said Shanti, smiling at her.

"Good. I knew Cora would enjoy it much more with her besties there!" said Helena. "It's great you can come."

"Mummy, look!" said Mollie May, spotting a display of dolls in the window of a nearby shop. She dragged her mum over to look at them.

Cora hung back and her friends slowed to keep pace with her. "Thanks for coming. I couldn't face being alone

with Horrible Helena and Mollie May."
She'd texted her friends to tell them what
she'd overheard at the stables, and they'd
agreed to meet her at the shopping
centre.

Sophie bit her lip. "Cora, don't get mad
. . . but do you think you might have
misunderstood what you heard?

Emily nodded. "Maybe you're upset
because of your mum? I mean, I found
it weird enough when my mum got
together with Dave, and she and Dad
were only divorced. It must be even
harder for you."

"It's not about my mum!" Cora said,
tears springing to her eyes. "I just don't

want Dad getting hurt, OK?"

"OK," said Emily slowly. "But you're absolutely sure you heard Helena say those things yesterday?"

"Yes!" insisted Cora. "She's planning on dumping Dad soon after she marries him!"

"I can't believe it; she seems so nice," whispered Shanti, glancing over at Helena.

"She's not nice, she's horrible!" said Cora.

"Come on, girls!" called Helena, beckoning them over. "Our appointment is in five minutes. We don't want to be late for it!"

Much to Cora's surprise, trying on the dresses was really good fun. There was no one else in the bridesmaid section of the shop apart from them and the sales assistant, Valerie. When Mollie May dragged Helena to the rail of dresses for younger girls, Valerie went with them and let Cora, Shanti, Sophie and Emily go into a big changing room and try things on by themselves.

"Well, what do you think?" Cora said, flouncing out from behind a curtain and striking a pose. She had chosen a mint green dress with layers and layers of lace.

It frothed out around her.

"You look like a waterfall!" said Shanti.

"Or Princess Fiona in *Shrek*," giggled Emily, who was trying on an enormous blue hat with a huge brim that she had found on a hat stand.

"Well, you look like you've got a spaceship on your head!" Cora retorted, with a grin.

"You could wear this and pretend to be a snow queen," said Shanti, swirling round in a white, fake fur cloak. "After all, the wedding is taking place in a castle! Or . . ." She picked up a hat that had some plastic grapes and an apple on

the brim. "You could go disguised as a
fruit bowl!"

"I think this is the dress for you!" said
Sophie, coming out from her changing
cubicle wearing a bright pink dress with
fake diamonds all over it.

"Oh yes, it's just so you, Cora," said
Emily, grinning.

Helena poked her head into the
changing room. "Have you found
anything you like?" She saw the dress
Cora was wearing. "Please tell me that's
not under serious consideration."

"No, it's just a joke," she admitted.

"Phew!" said Helena. "Well, what do
you think of this one?"

Cora tensed as Helena held up a dress. She was expecting it to be some pink poofy creation, but it was a long dress made from a soft shimmering pale blue fabric with a narrow velvet ribbon around the waist.

"Try it on," Helena urged her. "It's your favourite colour."

"Ooh yes, go on," said Sophie. "I bet it'll look really nice on you."

Cora took it. "I don't look good in dresses," she grumbled from inside the changing room as she got into it.

She came out and everyone gasped.

"Oh, wow! It's gorgeous!" said Emily.

"Stunning!" said Sophie.

Shanti nodded hard.

Helena beamed. "I knew it would suit you, Cora. Well, what do you think?" She motioned to the mirror. Cora stepped over and looked at her reflection. She hardly recognised herself. She looked so different to normal but the others were right. The dress did suit her, and she liked the way the fabric felt floaty and light. "I . . . I like it," she said, in surprise.

"The blue matches your eyes perfectly," said Helena.

Cora stepped closer to the mirror. "Dad says I've got Mum's eyes."

"They're beautiful," said Helena softly. "And I'm sure he'd love to see you in

that dress. Should we make that your bridesmaid dress then?"

Cora glanced up at her. "But what about Mollie May? She's not going to want to wear blue. She likes pink."

Helena winked. "Leave it to me."

She left the changing room and went over to the rails. Cora saw her pick out a younger girl's version of the blue dress. It had a fuller skirt and puffier sleeves but was made of the same shimmering blue fabric. "Molsy?" Helena called. "Come and see this pretty dress."

Mollie May came running over. She saw the dress and her face fell. "But it's not pink," she protested.

Helena shook the dress out, showing its full skirt. "I know, but Cora doesn't like pink and I want everyone to be happy at the wedding. If you wore this one, you'd look just like Cinderella when she dances with Prince Charming at the ball." She looked over her shoulder. "Cora, come and show Mollie May what your dress looks like so she can see how lovely it is."

Cora stepped out from behind the curtain and Mollie May's eyes widened. "You look really pretty!" She turned to her mum. "I want to look like Cinderella too."

"Let's pop it on you and see how it looks then," said Helena, going into a

changing cubicle with her.

When Mollie May came out a few minutes later, she was beaming. She spun round in her dress, making the full skirt twirl around her. "Look at me!" she cried happily as she danced round the shop floor.

"You look just like Cinderella," Sophie told her.

Mollie May skipped over to Cora.

"You look gorgeous together," said Helena. "So, that's decided, we've chosen the bridesmaid dresses."

Mollie May took Cora's hand. "You know what I really want as well," she said to her. "I want a carriage pulled

by a white horse just like real princesses
have. Can Star pull a carriage?"

"No, he's not big enough," said Cora.

"But at the stables there's a carriage they hire out for weddings with two horses that are trained to pull it."

"Mummy!" Mollie May cried. "Can we go to the wedding in a carriage?"

"Well, I was actually thinking about going in a big silver car," said Helena.

"But that's boring!" said Mollie May, pouting. "I want to go in a carriage." She ran over and looked up at Helena through her curly eyelashes. "Please, Mummy. Pleeeeease?"

Helena hesitated. "All right," she said at last. "I'll talk to the owner of the stables and see if it's possible."

"Yay!" Mollie May said, skipping

happily. "It's going to be the best wedding ever!"

Helena smiled and caught her by the waist, swinging her round. "It is, isn't it? And afterwards we're all going to live happily ever after!"

Her words brought Cora back to reality with a thump. *Happily ever after.* Helena's happily ever after was definitely not the same one her dad was imagining. She obviously just wanted Dad's money.

Cora's mouth tightened and she marched back into the changing room. She pulled the blue dress off over her head. What was she thinking, getting

excited about horses and carriages and dresses? This wedding wasn't going to go ahead – it couldn't.

*I've GOT to find a way to stop it,* she thought with a rush of determination.

# Chapter Four

A quick text to her dad and then to the other parents resulted in the Bridesmaids Club going to Cora's house for a sleepover that night. Cora really wanted a chance to talk properly to the others and see if they could help her come up with some ideas for how she could stop

the wedding from going ahead.

On the way home, Helena drove to everyone's houses so they could pick up the things they needed, then she took them to the supermarket so they could choose some snacks. "Get whatever you want to eat," she told everyone. "My treat."

Cora saw her friends swapping looks. She could tell they were thinking how nice Helena was and she felt a rush of frustration. Helena was so good at acting as if she was kind and generous. *But she's just pretending,* thought Cora darkly.

When they got home, Dad was in the kitchen. There was a large bouquet of white lilies in a vase on the kitchen table. "For you!" he said, smiling at Helena and gesturing to the bouquet with a flourish. "My favourite flowers for my beautiful fiancée."

"Oh, thanks!' said Helena. "They're ... lovely, Joe."

Cora frowned as she caught a false note in Helena's voice. As Dad turned away, she noticed Helena pull a face and step back from the flowers.

"I thought I'd save you a job on the wedding list. After I stopped at the caterer's, I went into *Blooms and Blossoms* to talk about the flowers for the wedding," Dad said cheerfully.

"I've always loved Christmas lilies so I suggested those as we're getting married in December. What do you think?"

"Lilies . . ."

Helena bit her lip. "Is there a problem?" Dad said. "They're ringing tomorrow to confirm we want to go ahead with the order, so you can change it then."

Helena smiled and shook her head. "No, no, of course there's not a problem. If they're your favourites, we should

definitely have Christmas lilies."

Dad beamed and kissed her.

Cora turned quickly away. "Anyone want a drink?" she asked tightly. "Come and see what we've got." She threw open the fridge and her friends joined her to pick cans of fizzy drinks.

"We're going to have a carriage and two horsies at the wedding," said Mollie May.

"A carriage?" echoed Dad. He looked at Helena. "I thought we were having a limo?"

"We were, but Mollie really wants me to ride in a carriage," said Helena, shrugging her shoulders.

"Like a real princess," Mollie May put in happily.

"Cora said the stables have a carriage with two horses that can be hired for weddings," said Helena. "Is that OK?"

"Sure." Dad chuckled and shook his head. "Goodness me, though – a castle *and* a carriage. We'll have to sell the house at this rate!"

Cora stared. He didn't mean that, did he?

Helena smiled and kissed him. "It'll all be worth it when we have the perfect wedding day," she said.

"Yes, that's all I want too," said Dad, kissing her back.

Cora marched to the kitchen door. "Come on," she said to her friends abruptly. "Let's go upstairs."

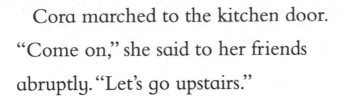

Soon, they were all in Cora's room, sitting on her big double bed. "She doesn't love Dad, she's just pretending," Cora said angrily. "But what can I do? How can I stop the wedding?"

"I think you should talk to your dad about what you heard," said Shanti.

"He wouldn't believe me," said Cora, shaking her head. "And if he asked Helena about it, she'd probably just make up some excuse and lie."

"Could you get proof?" said Sophie. "Trick her into saying something and record her using your phone."

"I could try . . ." said Cora, wondering how she could make that happen.

"I just can't believe it," said Emily, shaking her head. "She seems so nice. It must all be an act."

There was a knock at the door and Helena looked in. "Girls, Cora's dad brought home a candy-floss maker and a chocolate fountain from the caterers so we can decide which one to have at the wedding." She broke off to sneeze. "Do you want to help test them out?"

"Yes, please!" exclaimed Sophie, Shanti

74

and Emily. They jumped to their feet, pulling Cora up with them.

Helena grinned. "I thought you might. Come on then!" She sneezed again and led the way downstairs. "Go on in," she said, waving them through to the kitchen. "I need to nip out and buy some tablets to stop me sneezing." She picked up her car keys and phone and headed out.

Cora's dad was in the kitchen with a chocolate fountain machine on the table and a big bag of chocolate drops. "OK, let's try this one first," he said. "Actually, Cora, can you just run after Helena and ask her to pick up some strawberries while she's out. I bet they'll go really nicely with the chocolate."

Cora hurried outside. Helena was leaning against the car, talking on her phone. "I don't know what to do," Cora heard her saying. "I hate them, I really do, but I'm stuck with them." She broke off to sneeze and spotted Cora. "Oh, hi, Cora."

Cora woodenly repeated her dad's message. So Helena hated her and Dad, did she? But she felt she was stuck with them?

*Well, not if I have anything to do with it,* thought Cora, turning and marching away.

The Bridesmaids Club and Mollie May
had great fun trying out the chocolate
fountain and candy-floss machine. The
thick, gooey chocolate tasted delicious
with strawberries and marshmallows.
The candy-floss machine produced
lots of fluffy pink candy floss that they
caught on sticks. They all got very sticky
and had to have showers before they
changed into their pyjamas.

"I wish we could keep the chocolate
fountain and the candy-floss machine,"
Mollie May said as Helena took her
upstairs to read her a bedtime story.

"I think you'd be at the dentist having a filling every week if we did," laughed Helena. "Now, come on, time to brush your teeth."

Up in Cora's room, with their blow-up beds laid out on the floor, the Bridesmaids Club tried to think of ways Cora could trick Helena into saying how she really felt while recording her with her phone. In the end, they gave up and played Consequences and "Would You Rather".

"We've still not thought up a plan to stop the wedding," said Cora as they all snuggled down in their sleeping bags.

"We'll think about it . . . in the

morning," yawned Emily.

"Yeah, in the morning," agreed Sophie sleepily.

"Night, Cora," said Shanti.

"Night," Cora mumbled. Her friends might be tired but Cora was sure she wasn't going to be able to fall asleep. She had too much to think about. The conversations she'd overheard Helena having . . . the way Helena had looked at Dad's flowers . . . Worrying thoughts swirled through her mind as she lay in bed, but eventually her eyes shut and the next moment she was fast asleep.

## Chapter Five

After Cora's friends had gone home
the next day, Helena headed out to the
shops. She came back laden with bags.
"Looks like you've been busy!" Dad
said, helping her carry the bags into the
lounge.

"What have you bought, Mummy?

Anything for me?" asked Mollie May in excitement.

"Maybe a few things," said Helena with a smile. "But they're not for now, they're for Christmas," she went on quickly as Mollie May ran to the bags. "So, no peeking. I also got some new decorations for the Christmas tree."

"But the tree's already decorated," said Cora. They'd put the tree up and decorated it the previous weekend.

"I know but I don't really like the way it looks," said Helena.

Cora glanced at the Christmas tree. It was decorated with the ornaments that Cora and her dad had always used, but also with the decorations that Helena and Mollie May had brought with them when they moved in. The two sets really didn't go together – Helena and Mollie May's were all bright pink, purple and silver, while Helena and her dad's were mostly red and gold. There were also lots of home-made things, too – wonky stockings cut out of felt, gold stars made from pipe cleaners and a white snowman made from cardboard and covered with glitter. Cora had made them with her mum when she was little.

"Ta da!" Helena pulled out several boxes of silver and white decorations. There were baubles and fairy lights, delicate glass icicles and white china fairies. "I thought we needed some brand-new decorations for our brand-new family!" She beamed.

Mollie May squealed with delight. "They're so pretty, Mummy!"

"What a great idea! And this way we get the fun of decorating the tree all over again!" said Dad, kissing Helena.

Mollie May ran over to the tree and started pulling off the old decorations. She threw the precious snowman on the ground.

"No!" cried Cora. This was the final straw. "Stop it! Stop it!" she shouted at Mollie May.

Mollie May swung round, her eyes alarmed.

"Whoa, Cora! Calm down!" her dad said.

Cora grabbed the snowman decoration from the floor, feeling furious. "I don't want new decorations. I want the old ones we've always had."

"That's fine," said Helena. "I'm

not saying we should throw the old decorations away, Cora. You could use them to decorate your bedroom. We can even get you a little Christmas tree of your own. That way, you get to keep the decorations you like upstairs and the tree down here will look lovely. It's a win-win."

*You mean, it's a win for you,* Cora thought, tears suddenly prickling in her eyes. *This way you get to wipe Mum out of the picture, making it seem like she never existed.*

"What do you say, Cora?" asked Dad. She could tell he was desperate for her not to make a fuss.

"Fine," she said tightly, not wanting to upset him. "But *I'll* take my decorations off the tree!" she added, glaring at Mollie May.

"Mols, why don't you come and help me make some hot chocolate?" said Helena. "Then we can all redecorate the tree when Cora's finished."

Cora carefully removed her decorations, packed them into a box and carried them upstairs. She sat down on her bed with its blue duvet cover. Unhappiness swirled through her as she looked down at the snowman's smiling face. *Oh, Mum,* she thought unhappily, *I wish you were still here.*

After they had put the supper dishes in
the dishwasher, Cora and Dad snuggled
down on the big squashy sofa to watch
a film together. Sunday night was film
night – it had been a tradition ever since
Cora had been tiny. She and Dad still
made Mum's special buttered popcorn
and shared a big bowl between them.
Helena never stayed to watch a film
with them, she always went upstairs to
'have some me-time'.

"This is nice," said Cora, cuddling
closer against her dad's side. Her
favourite times were when it was just the

two of them, alone like this.

"It is," her dad said, dropping a kiss on the top of her head.

Cora glanced up at him. Maybe she could talk to him now? If she could persuade him not to get married to Helena then that would solve everything.

"Dad," she said slowly.

"Yes, poppet?"

"Um." Cora lips felt suddenly dry. She licked them. "Are you sure you're doing the right thing marrying Helena?"

He frowned. "What's brought this on?"

"It's just, are you sure she really loves you?" Cora asked him.

The worried look on her dad's face

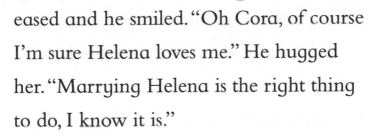

eased and he smiled. "Oh Cora, of course I'm sure Helena loves me." He hugged her. "Marrying Helena is the right thing to do, I know it is."

Cora took a deep breath. "But what if she leaves you?"

Her dad smiled. "I really don't think that's going to happen."

"But—" Cora began.

Dad put a finger gently on her lips and interrupted her. "Cora, I know you miss your mum. I do too – part of me always will. But Helena and I make each other happy and I really can't wait to marry her and for us all to be a family. Now, come on, let's relax and watch this film."

He pressed *play* and the film started.
Cora watched the opening titles, barely
taking them in.

If she couldn't make Dad see the truth
then there was only one thing for it – she
was going to have to stop the wedding
herself!

The next day, after school, Cora was
pouring herself a glass of blackcurrant
squash when there was a knock at the
door. Helena was out at work, Mollie
May was watching TV and Dad was in
his study, so Cora went to answer it. A
woman was standing on the doorstep

with two pale blue bridesmaid dresses on hangers. "Oh, hi," she said with a bright smile. "I'm from *Wedding Belles*. I'm just dropping these off for Helena Avery – it's the two bridesmaid dresses she bought."

"Oh, right, thanks," said Cora, taking the dresses. "I'll give them to her."

Cora carried the dresses through to the kitchen and put them on the table.

*I should probably take them upstairs,* she thought, *so they don't get dirty.*

Picking them and her glass of squash up, she set off upstairs but as she did so, she trod on one of Mollie May's princess dolls that had been left on the bottom step. "Ow!" she gasped, stumbling.

Blackcurrant squash flew into the air
and then splattered down on to the
dresses.

Cora froze. *Oh no!* She was about to
race back to the kitchen to get a cloth to
clean the juice off but then she paused.
Maybe *this* was how she could stop the

wedding. If she sabotaged everything she could – and Helena only found out on the morning of the wedding – then perhaps the ceremony would be called off? That would give her more time to show her dad what Helena was really like.

Cora hesitated and then she made her decision. She hurried upstairs and hung the dresses at the back of her wardrobe. Her heart pounded guiltily but she ignored it. She wanted to stop the wedding, didn't she? Maybe she could spoil Helena's dress, too? No, it was still at the shop, she remembered. They wanted to do a final fitting a few days

before the wedding and make any last-minute alterations to its size then so that it looked perfect on the day.

*But what about Helena's wedding shoes?* thought Cora.

Helena's wedding shoes had high heels and were made of silk, encrusted with tiny crystals. Cora's dad had bought them for Helena after she'd found them online. Cora couldn't imagine ever wanting to wear shoes like that but Mollie May had squealed in delight and said they were like Cinderella's shoes. She'd wanted to try them on but Helena had said no, they were much too expensive. She'd laughed and said that if

it rained, she was going to have to wear wellies to the castle and then change into her shoes when she got inside to make sure they didn't get ruined before she'd even walked down the aisle.

Cora tiptoed down the landing to Dad and Helena's room. She went inside and opened the wardrobe. On the shoe rack there was a white box embossed with silver writing. Cora opened it and saw the sparkling shoes. What could she do to them? She thought for a moment, then went into the bathroom and held the shoes under the tap until they were soaking wet. Then she shoved them in the box and put them back into Helena's

wardrobe. One pair of wedding shoes ruined!

Just as she was wondering if there was anything else she could do, the home telephone rang. Cora answered it.

"Hello, could I speak to Mr Hopkinson or Ms Avery please?" a woman said. "It's Lorna calling from *Blooms and Blossom*. I'm ringing to get confirmation on the order for the wedding."

As the florist spoke, an idea came to Cora – a daring, but brilliant idea. Could she really go ahead with it?

"Oh, hello," she said, trying to sound grown-up. "This is Helena Avery. I'm afraid I've decided to cancel the order."

"Oh dear," the florist said, sounding surprised. "I'm sorry to hear that."

"Yes, I really don't like Christmas lilies."

"Well, if you do want us to do the flowers for the wedding you'll need to place a new order within the next forty-eight hours. After that, we can't guarantee we'll be able to fulfil the order."

"I'll think about it. Goodbye." Cora put the phone down. Her heart was thumping hard and the breath felt short in her chest. What had she just done?

Pushing aside the doubts that were beginning to form, she reminded herself

that it was for the best. She'd wanted to find a way to stop the wedding, and now she had. And when Helena revealed her true colours, Dad would thank her for it!

## Chapter Six

"Did either of you take in the bridesmaid dresses from *Wedding Belles* today?" Helena said to Cora and her dad as the three of them ate creamy pasta carbonara for supper that night. Mollie May had eaten earlier and was already tucked up in bed.

"I did," said Cora. "I put them in my wardrobe to keep them safe."

"Thanks, sweetie," said Helena. "That's one less thing to worry about." She rubbed her forehead. "Oh dear, work's been very stressful today. I told you about that shipment of hideous purple shoes that got delivered. I've been trying to work out what to do with them . . ."

As Helena started to talk about boring work stuff, Cora tuned out and thought about Star. She only started paying attention again when she heard the words "horse" and "stables".

"So, I'll pick you up tomorrow after school, Cora sweetie, and we'll go to the

stables together then?"

Cora frowned. "Why? Dad usually picks me up on Tuesdays."

Dad got up to clear the plates away and fetch pudding. "Haven't you been listening? Helena said she wants to sort out the carriage tomorrow, so she's going to call in and see Annabeth."

"I've spoken to her on the phone already so I just need to pay the deposit to secure the booking," Helena said to Cora. "I might as well drop you off at the same time."

Cora nodded. "OK."

"I'll give you the deposit, Cora, and you can give it to her," said Helena.

"Sure," Cora said. Another idea had just popped into her head. Maybe she could tell Annabeth that Helena had changed her mind and wanted to cancel the carriage?

"Annabeth said she'll show me the horses who'll pull the carriage." Helena didn't sound keen. "But I'm not sure that's necessary."

"You'll have to be careful if you do. Duke and Duchess sometimes bite and kick," Cora lied.

Helena's face paled. "Really? Is it safe for them to be used as carriage horses then?"

"Oh, they only bite the bride if they

don't like her," said Cora mischievously.

Helena swallowed. "Oh," she said in a small voice.

"It would probably be best not to take any chances," said Cora.

Helena nodded quickly. "Good thinking," she said, then she jumped up to help Cora's dad.

"Well, here we are," said Helena as she parked at the stables the next day after school. Mollie May had gone to a friend's house for tea so it was just the two of them. Helena had been very quiet on the drive to the stables. A couple of times, she had opened her mouth as if about to say something but then seemed to change her mind.

Cora was puzzled. Helena was usually very chatty. Why was she acting so strangely? Did she suspect that Cora was trying to stop the wedding?

Cora got out of the car. "Shall I take the deposit and give it to Annabeth?" she said.

Helena hesitated. "I don't know. I've been thinking about it ... Maybe I should see these horses first."

"Oh no, don't worry about that," Cora said quickly. "You're not exactly dressed for walking around a stables." Helena was wearing high-heeled shoes along with skinny white jeans.

"I'm not, am I?" Helena paused and then made up her mind. A look of relief crossed her face. "You're right. It's a silly idea to get out. I'll come back and pick you up later. Here's the deposit." She handed Cora an envelope. "Can you give it to Annabeth for me and confirm the booking?"

"Sure," said Cora. She watched Helena drive off then stuck the envelope in her pocket and headed to Star's stable. She wasn't going to give the deposit to Annabeth. In fact, when she saw her, she was going to tell her that Helena had changed her mind!

Cora groomed Star and tacked him up. She took him out through the car park and into the riding arena where she spent a lovely hour riding. When she finished, she dismounted and led Star back to his stable. To her surprise Helena's car was already waiting in the car park.

Cora led Star over to the car but there was no sign of Helena inside.

"Cora!" Hearing her name, Cora turned. Annabeth, an older woman with grey hair in a ponytail, was on a small tractor moving a massive bale of hay. "Are you looking for Helena?" she

called, switching the tractor engine off
for a moment so they could talk.

Cora nodded. "Yes, where is she?"

"She came to find me. She said you've
got the deposit money for the carriage."

"Oh, yeah." Cora felt her heart sink
as she realised she couldn't carry out
her plan now. "Um, here it is." She led
Star over to the tractor and handed the
envelope to Annabeth.

"Thanks." Annabeth chuckled. "I'm
not sure Helena knows very much about
horses, does she? She seemed worried
Duke and Duchess were going to bite
her! I told her they're gentle giants and
she could go and pat them if she liked.

She'll probably be round by their stables."

"OK, thanks, Annabeth," said Cora.

She led Star to the stable block. As she turned the corner, she saw Helena by Duke's stable. He was looking over the door, his grey ears pricked, as Helena talked to him.

"There's a good horsey," she was saying, her voice higher than normal. "I'm just going to pat your nose. Don't bite me, please!"

Cora bit back a grin as Helena teetered forward on her high-heeled shoes and gingerly reached out a hand. Duke chose just that moment to snort.

Helena shrieked and jumped

backwards. Her shoes slipped and she fell over, arms windmilling as she landed in a pile of horse poo!

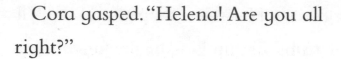

Cora gasped. "Helena! Are you all right?"

She led Star forward, reaching out her hand to help Helena up, but as she got closer, Helena shrank back. "No! No! Please keep him away from me!" Her face was pale.

Cora paused. Helena looked terrified! Her eyes widened as she realised something. It wasn't that Helena didn't like horses – she was *scared* of them.

"Wait a sec. I'll tie Star up." Cora led Star over to his stable and quickly put his headcollar on. Leaving him safely tied up, she hurried back to Helena. Her stepmother-to-be's head was buried in

her arms and she was sobbing.

Cora bit her lip. She'd never seen Helena cry before. She crouched down beside her. "Are . . . are you OK?" she asked.

"No," Helena sobbed. "I don't know how I'm going to go through with this. How can I have a horse and carriage at my wedding when I'm terrified of horses?"

"I don't understand," Cora said. "Why did you agree in the first place if you're so scared? Oh, I get it," she suddenly realised. "It's because it's a fancy thing to do, right?"

"No!" Helena exclaimed. "I said we

could have a horse and carriage because that's what Mollie May really wanted!" Helena raised her tear-filled eyes to Cora's. "I agreed because I wanted Mollie May to be happy, just like I agreed to have blue bridesmaid dresses because I know you love blue even though my favourite colour is red. And I really wanted roses, but I agreed to have lilies, even though I'm allergic to them, because they're your dad's favourite flowers. I said yes to all those things because I want everyone to be happy. It's costing me a fortune but it will be worth it if everyone has a perfect day!"

"It's costing *you* a fortune?" Cora

echoed. "Don't you mean it's costing Dad a fortune?"

Helena frowned. "Your dad? No? I'm paying for most of the wedding. He bought the shoes for me – and we're splitting the cost of the food and drink – but I'm paying for everything else. I'd never spend so much if I was asking your dad to pay for it all."

Cora felt like she had when she'd been on a massive rollercoaster and it had suddenly dropped downwards. "But I thought Dad was the rich one ..."

Helena stared at her. "Cora, my business is very successful. I actually earn more than him." Her forehead crinkled

and a look of realisation filled her eyes.
"Did you think I'm marrying your dad
for his money?"

Cora nodded slowly.

"No," Helena said, shaking her head.
"No, no, no. I promise you, I'm marrying
your dad because I love him. That's the
only reason."

"But I don't understand!" Cora said. "I
heard you talking on the phone! Twice!
The first time you said you were going
to get the money and get out fast. The
second time you said you hated us but
had to put up with us – for now."

Helena looked confused – and then
horrified. "Oh, Cora, I wasn't talking

about getting married. I was talking
about the shipment of awful purple shoes
I have in right now. I hate them and
want to get rid of them as fast as possible
so I can get some of my money back."
She studied Cora's face. "I can't believe
you thought I hated you and your dad.
No wonder you don't like me."

Cora sank back on to her heels. She
didn't know what to say. She'd got it
all so wrong. A wave of guilt hit her
as she thought about everything she'd
done – ruining the dresses and the shoes,
cancelling the flowers. Tears sprang to
her eyes and she felt like she was going
to be sick. "Oh," she said in a small voice.

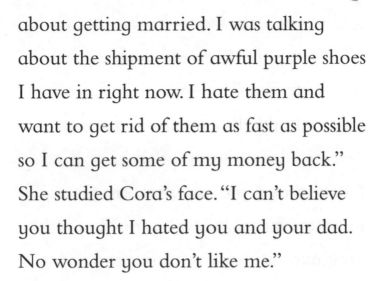

She covered her face with her hands.

"What is it?" Helena asked.

"I've done some really bad things," Cora whispered through her fingers. "Helena, I told you that Duke and Duchess were vicious when they're really just big softies. Duke wasn't trying to bite you just now, he was just snorting. It's what all horses do."

"That's OK," said Helena.

Cora shook her head. "That isn't the worst of it. I spilled some squash on the bridesmaid dresses and stained them. It was an accident, but then I decided not to tell you because I thought if you found out they were ruined on the day

of the wedding, it might stop it from going ahead. I also cancelled the flowers and," she swallowed hard, "I . . . I ruined your wedding shoes." She stared down at her knees, unable to meet Helena's eyes. "I'm really sorry."

There was a moment of silence and then she felt Helena squeeze her arm. Cora looked up into Helena's eyes.

"It's OK. You thought I was trying to hurt your dad and so you wanted to stop the wedding from happening. I get it. I do. You were only trying to protect him." Helena took a breath and let it out in a rush. "How do you feel about me marrying your dad now?"

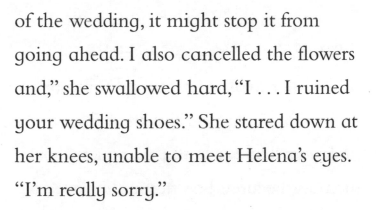

Cora hesitated. Was she OK with it?

When she didn't answer, Helena studied her face. "Is it because of your mum, Cora? Do you feel that you and your dad are being disloyal to her memory because he's getting married to me?"

Cora nodded slowly. Helena had put her feelings into words. "Yes," she muttered. "I feel like she's being forgotten."

"Oh, Cora," said Helena. "Your dad loves your mum and she isn't being forgotten, I promise. I understand how you're feeling, I really do." She stroked Cora's back. "I lost my mum when I was nineteen but I still think about her every single day. I promise I'll help you make sure your mum's remembered and never forgotten."

Cora felt something lift inside her as she met Helena's eyes. She could tell Helena understood – *really* understood.

Helena's arms opened and they hugged. When they finally separated, Helena gave Cora a serious look.

"So, now, let me ask you again – are you really OK with me marrying your dad, Cora? Because if you're not, then we'll call the wedding off for now. I mean it."

"No, don't do that," said Cora. "I want

you to get married!" She could hardly believe she was saying the words, but she realised she really and truly meant them.

Helena smiled. "Then the wedding will go ahead."

"But what about everything I've done?" said Cora.

"It can all be fixed, I'm sure," said Helena. "But I'll need you to help me sort things out."

Cora grinned. "OK, but first, you might want to go home and get changed."

Helena cast a rueful glance at her filthy white jeans. "I think that might be a good idea," she said, smiling.

Cora jumped up and helped Helena to her feet. It was time to put a new plan into action. Instead of stopping the wedding, she needed to save it!

## Chapter Seven

**Can you all come round to mine for an hour? I've got SO much to tell you! I definitely need some BC help!!!! Cxxx**

Cora sent the text to the rest of the Bridesmaids Club on the way home. Texts came pinging back as Emily, Sophie and Shanti promised they would

be at her house as soon as possible.

When they were back at home, Cora showed Helena the ruined bridesmaid dresses and shoes. "I'm really, really sorry," she added, feeling awful as Helena looked at the blackcurrant splashes on the dresses and at the water-stained white silk shoes.

Helena took a deep breath. "It's OK. We can sort this out. I've got an old pair of white pumps I can wear. They're plain, but I bet they'll be a lot comfier and better for dancing in than these ones would have been," she said, picking up the ruined high-heeled shoes. "And I've got a friend in the fashion business

who might be able to help with the bridesmaid dresses. But before I go and see him, I'd better shower so I don't smell like horse poo!"

Cora's friends arrived as Helena was showering.

"So, what's going on?" Sophie demanded as Cora let them in.

She took them into the kitchen and as they shared a packet of chocolate biscuits, she told them everything that had happened.

"So Helena isn't just marrying your dad for his money?" said Shanti.

"No, she loves him," said Cora. "In fact, she loves him so much she was going to

sneeze all through the wedding just so he could have the flowers he liked."

"I'm so glad you found out the truth," said Emily.

"So *Plan: Stop the Wedding* is off then?" said Sophie.

"Yep," Cora declared. "It's now *Plan: Save the Wedding*!"

"So, what do you want us to do?" asked Sophie.

"Help me fix things," said Cora. "Pleeeeease?"

Shanti grinned. "Of course we will! That's what the Bridesmaids Club is for!"

"Great! First, we need to sort the flowers out," said Cora.

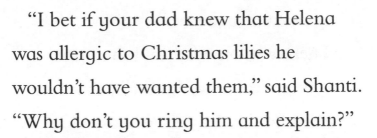

"I bet if your dad knew that Helena was allergic to Christmas lilies he wouldn't have wanted them," said Shanti. "Why don't you ring him and explain?"

Taking a deep breath, Cora rang her dad and told him what she had done.

"Oh, Cora-Flora," he said, sighing. "I wish you'd just talked to me about what you were thinking."

"I'm really sorry, Dad," said Cora quietly. And she meant it with all her heart.

"Well, I'd better call the florist and place the order again," he said.

"Wait, Dad!" said Cora. "Did you know that Helena is allergic to lilies?

They make her sneeze."

"Then why on earth did she agree to have them at the wedding?"

"Because she wanted to make you happy," explained Cora. "But really she wanted roses."

"Leave it with me," said her dad. "I'll call the florist and order roses."

"Red ones," added Cora. "Because that's her favourite colour."

Just after Cora had said goodbye to her dad, Helena came into the kitchen. She noticed the rest of the Bridesmaids Club. "Oh hi, girls."

"I've been telling everyone what's been happening," said Cora.

"And we're here to help!" said Emily.

"Well, I feel much better now I don't smell of horse poo any more. I don't know how you can bear that smell, Cora," said Helena.

"It's not too bad as long as you don't sit down in it!" said Cora, with a grin.

Helena laughed. "I must have looked pretty funny. I jumped a mile when that horse tried to bite me," she told the others.

"He didn't try to bite her," Cora said. "He was just snorting."

Helena shivered. "He sounded like a dragon."

"You're really scared of horses, aren't

you?" said Sophie curiously. "Why?"

"When I was four, we went on holiday to the countryside. I went into a field near the cottage and three horses trotted towards me. All I can remember is the sound of their hooves and them getting closer and closer. I turned and ran and ended up in a pile of nettles. I've been scared of horses ever since. I really wish Mollie May hadn't asked for a carriage at the wedding."

"Couldn't you tell her you don't want one?" said Shanti.

"I could but she'd be so upset," said Helena. "I'll just have to get through it as best I can. Now, let's deal with the things

that *can* be sorted out. I'll ring the florist and order the flowers."

"Way ahead of you," said Cora, grinning. "I called Dad and told him that you're allergic to lilies. So he's calling the florist to order red roses instead."

"Oh, wow!" said Helena. "Did he really not mind?"

"Not at all," said Cora.

"Thank you so much, sweetie!" said Helena. "I love red roses. Your dad bought them for me on our first date."

Cora smiled. The affection in Helena's voice was real. How could she have ever thought she was just pretending?

"I'd better go and see if I can save the bridesmaid dresses." Helena picked up her mobile and headed out.

"That leaves us with the shoes to sort out," said Sophie.

"Helena says she has an old pair of white pumps," said Cora. "But I know she wanted sparkly shoes."

"Then it's time to give them a Bridesmaids Club makeover!" said Emily.

Cora gave her a confused look. "A what?"

"You said you have some art supplies," said Emily. Cora nodded, still wondering what Emily was going on about. "Have you got any sequins?"

"I think so," said Cora, her eyes
starting to widen as she began to follow
Emily's train of thought.

"Then let's decorate Helena's old
shoes!" said Emily.

The Bridesmaids Club set to work.
They spread out newspaper and dug
out all the silver sequins and gems that
Cora had. Emily, who was brilliant at
art, sketched a design on paper then the
others started to stick the glittery gems
and sequins on to the shoes with fabric
glue. By the time they had finished,
the pumps were unrecognisable. They
sparkled and looked like new.

"Perfect!" Emily exclaimed.

"I hope Helena likes them," said Cora.
They didn't have to wait long to find
out. The girls had just tidied away the
craft things when Helena came back.

"Look what my friend gave me!" she
said, pulling two beautiful red dresses out
of a large bag. They had shimmering

skirts and their bodices and short sleeves were covered with sequins. "They're new designs he's been working on – you'll be the first to wear them."

"Oh, wow!" said Cora.

"They're beautiful!" said Shanti.

"And perfect for a Christmas wedding," said Sophie, smiling.

"We've been busy too," said Cora, taking Helena's hand and pulling her into the kitchen. "These are for you!" She pointed to the sparkling wedding shoes.

"Where did they come from?" said Helena in astonishment.

"They're yours!" said Cora.

"We gave your old shoes a makeover," said Emily.

Helena beamed. "Girls, I can't thank you enough! Everything is working out. The wedding is going to be even more perfect than it was before!" She went upstairs to hang up the dresses.

But something was still bothering Cora.

"It's not perfect, though," she told her friends. "Helena really doesn't want to travel in a horse and carriage."

"She said Mollie May will be upset if she doesn't," said Shanti.

Sophie scratched her head. "That might be a problem we can't fix."

"Unless . . ." Cora's eyes lit up. "Unless I can stop Helena being scared of horses. If I can do that, then everything will be perfect after all!"

# Chapter Eight

"Cora, are you quite sure about this?" Helena said nervously as Cora led her across the stable yard on Sunday. Mollie May skipped beside them.

"Absolutely!" Cora declared. "I'm going to prove to you that horses and ponies aren't scary. We'll start with

Star." She'd made sure that Helena was wearing sensible clothes that day – dark jeans, a long-sleeved old T-shirt and wellies. Helena had insisted on adding to the look with a diamanté belt and a silk scarf tied around her neck, and her purple wellies had a slight heel.

Star was looking over his stable door and he whinnied when he saw them. Helena stopped and shrank back.

"Mummy! Don't be silly. He's just saying hello!" said Mollie May, going up to Star. "He wants a treat."

Cora gave Mollie May a chunk of carrot and she fed it to him. "You have a go, Mummy!" Mollie May said.

"Yes, come on, Helena," Cora encouraged her.

Helena swallowed and walked up to Star. Cora gave her a piece of carrot. "Hold your hand flat and still," she instructed. "And let him take it from you."

"What if he bites me?" said Helena.

"He won't," said Cora.

She helped Helena hold her hand out and Star gently took the carrot.

"You can stroke him," said Cora.

Helena hesitated for a moment, but then she stroked Star's face. "He actually smells nice," she said.

"Pony is my favourite smell," said

Cora, kissing Star's
velvety cheek.
"It was my
mum's too.
She used
to say she
wished she
could bottle it
and have it as a
perfume."

"I wouldn't quite go that far but it is
surprisingly nice," said Helena. "Is that
one of the reasons you like coming to
the stables so much – they remind you of
your mum?"

Cora nodded. "I always feel close to

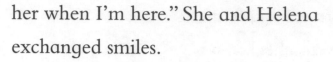

her when I'm here." She and Helena exchanged smiles.

Cora put Star's headcollar on and brought him out of the stable and showed Mollie May and Helena how to groom him. She held the brush in the hand closest to Star's head and swept it over him in the direction of his hair, getting rid of the dirt and grease.

"You have to move slowly around horses, Mummy," Mollie May instructed. "And you shouldn't go too close to their back legs and hooves. That's right, isn't it, Cora?"

Cora nodded. "Even friendly horses might step on you by accident or jump

back if they get startled by a sudden
noise. There's no need to be scared,
though. You just need to be careful and
sensible around them." She watched as
Helena and Mollie May groomed Star.
He loved being brushed and he dozed
happily in the sun as they fussed over
him.

To finish off, Cora showed them how
to brush conditioning spray through
his tail and paint his hooves with oil to
make them shine.

Helena laughed. "I didn't know you
put nail varnish on horses! It's like he's
had a pedicure."

Cora smiled. Helena was definitely

looking more relaxed now.

"I love horsies, Mummy," said Mollie May, putting her arms round the pony's neck and burying her face in his mane. "I wish I could have riding lessons."

"Maybe you can," said Helena. "I was worried you might get hurt. But if you had a calm pony like Star to learn on, I'm sure it would be OK."

After finishing grooming Star, Cora asked Annabeth if she could get Duke out. Then she repeated the whole process with him, grooming the big horse with Helena and Mollie May.

"He's really gentle, isn't he?" said Helena, as she stroked Duke's face.

Duke nuzzled her and snorted gently but this time Helena didn't shriek, she just chuckled. "Yuck!" she said, wiping the droplets away.

Annabeth was passing by. "How about I get the carriage out and we go for a quick spin – it'll do Duke and Duchess good to get some exercise."

"Yes!" said Mollie May excitedly.

"Oh . . . OK, I guess," said Helena, shooting an anxious look at Cora.

"It'll be fun," Cora assured her.

A little while later, they were all sitting in the carriage as Duke and Duchess trotted along a country road, their hooves clip-clopping. The carriage was

open-topped, with a hood that could
be pulled up if the weather wasn't very
good. Helena and Mollie May sat on the
grey leather seat at the back together,
while Cora sat up at the front with
Annabeth, who was driving.

"What do you think?" Cora said,
looking round at Helena.

Helena smiled. "I'm enjoying it! Oh!"
Her eyes widened as Duke did a poo as
he was trotting along. "Oh, my goodness.
What if he does that at the wedding?"

Cora grinned. "He might."

Mollie May giggled. "Don't worry,
Mummy. It'll be funny if he does.
Everyone will just laugh."

Helena smiled. "I guess you're right,"
she said, then she relaxed back against
the seat as Duke and Duchess trotted on.

"So? Are you less scared of horses now?"
Cora said when they finally finished at
the stables and walked back to the car.

"I actually am," said Helena. "I think I'm going to enjoy riding to the wedding in the carriage." She put an arm round Cora's shoulders and hugged her. "Thank you for being so patient with me."

"No problem," said Cora. "It's been fun having you here – both of you," she said, including Mollie May with a smile. Her stepsister-to-be was much easier to get on with at the stables. She didn't have tantrums and she listened to what Cora said. The little girl obviously wanted to be helpful.

"Next time you come to the stables, I'll let you have a ride on Star," Cora said to Mollie May. "Then maybe you can

start having some proper lessons with Annabeth."

"Oh, yes!" said Mollie May. "And when I'm as big as Cora can I have my own pony, Mummy? Pleeeease!"

Helena ruffled her daughter's hair. "We'll see. Having a pony is a big responsibility. But if you have lessons and let Cora teach you how to look after a pony then maybe one day you can have your own. Now," she turned to Cora. "We've spent today doing your favourite thing – so how about next Sunday, we all do my favourite thing?"

"OK," Cora said slowly, her heart sinking. "You want us to go shopping."

"Well, actually, I was thinking about a spa day!" said Helena. "You, me, Mollie May and your friends from the Bridesmaids Club if they want to come along. A proper girly day out, my treat. We can have manicures and face masks and there are some seriously fun massage jets to use in the pool. What do you say? Does that sound like a good plan?"

"Oh, yes!" Cora exclaimed, smiling. "It really does!"

# Chapter Nine

"This is awesome!" said Sophie as the Bridesmaids Club stepped into the pool at the spa. The turquoise water was wonderfully warm and the sides of the pool were made from artificial rock. Tropical plants hung down from the ceiling. Around the sides of the pool there

were different massage jets – some that sent streams of water pummelling on to their shoulders, others that sent jets of water up from the bottom of the pool to massage the soles of their feet, and some that bubbled gently around their backs. There was also a cavern lit up by coloured spotlights where water cascaded over a ledge in a mini waterfall.

Beside the pool, there was a large round jacuzzi. Helena and Mollie May sat in the warm bubbles chatting and watching as the Bridesmaids Club swam around the pool, trying out the different massage jets.

"It's like being in the Amazon

rainforest!" gasped Shanti as she surfaced from swimming underwater and came up near a palm tree planted in a pot.

"I love this place!" said Emily.

Mollie May came to join them in the pool and they all pretended to be mermaids. Then they played sharks and fishes, taking it in turns to chase each other. Mollie May was as good as gold; she seemed to be loving being included with the big girls for the day.

"Time to get out and have our treatments!" called Helena at last.

They showered and put on white fluffy robes, then they went to the nail parlour. Sitting in big comfy chairs, they all had

their hands massaged with rose-scented hand cream and then their nails were filed and shaped by nail technicians. Finally, they got to choose the colour nail polish they wanted.

Helena opted for dark pink, Shanti chose glittering gold and Sophie picked a turquoise blue. Emily decided to have a different colour polish on each nail while Mollie May chose a bright bubblegum pink. Cora didn't know what colour to pick. She never usually wore nail polish. She didn't want anything too girly.

"How about this one?" suggested Helena, pointing out a bright red with golden glittering bits.

"That looks lovely on," said the nail technician.

"And it'll go really well with your bridesmaid dress," said Helena.

"I'll have that one then, please," said Cora.

It was the perfect choice. Her nails looked amazing afterwards. Everyone's did! While they waited for their nail polish to dry, they all got face masks that smelled like cucumber and made their skin feel really smooth afterwards.

When their treatments were done, they sat in a room that smelled of scented oils and drank tropical fruit smoothies while a waiter brought them a large tray of

little cupcakes and rainbow-coloured macaroons.

"Thank you for inviting us, Helena," said Sophie.

"Yes, thank you," chorused Shanti and Emily.

"I love spa days!" said Mollie May.

"So, what do you think, Cora?" Helena asked. "Do you approve?"

"I had no idea spa days could be so fun," Cora admitted, smiling.

"So, if I was to suggest that after the wedding, you, me and Mollie May could maybe start coming on a spa day once every couple of months as a treat, you'd say yes?" said Helena.

"I would – as long as you agreed to come to the stables and share my favourite thing sometimes too," said Cora.

"Oh, we'll definitely be doing that," said Helena. "I spoke to Annabeth yesterday and she's agreed to start giving Mollie May riding lessons every Sunday. Who knows? I might even ask if she can give me some lessons too!"

Cora felt a rush of happiness. Everything really was working out perfectly after all!

When they got home, Dad admired their

nails. "Very smart," he said. "Now, let's get supper on and then it's film night."

"Before we do that, I've been thinking," said Helena. "With all the wedding preparations, we haven't had time to get Cora a miniature Christmas tree for her room. How about you bring your decorations down, Cora, and we'll put them back on the tree?"

"But the tree only has white and silver decorations on it," said Cora. She had to admit, it did look really pretty.

Helena shrugged. "So? A bit of colour will liven it up. Go and get them."

Cora went upstairs. The old decorations were still in the box. She

hesitated as she looked at them. Cora
thought for a moment and then
picked up the white snowman
from the top. Leaving the
rest of the decorations in
the box, she took the
snowman downstairs.
"Maybe just this
one," she said,
hanging it
on the
tree.

It fitted in perfectly with the other silver and white decorations, but it was also a reminder of her mum, hanging there on the tree. She stood back and, catching Helena's eye, they shared a private smile.

"So, what are you two going to watch tonight?" Helena said.

"I'm not sure yet," said Dad. "Have you got any ideas, Cora?"

Cora frowned. She had always assumed Helena didn't join in with their film night because she didn't want to spend time with her. But now that she knew Helena better, she found herself wondering if she actually went off so that Cora and her dad could have some

time together, on their own. Maybe she wasn't being unfriendly, maybe she was being considerate?

"Well?" Dad said to Cora.

"Maybe we could all watch a film together," said Cora.

"But Sunday night is your special time with your dad," said Helena. "I don't want to intrude."

"It doesn't have to just be me and Dad. Film night could be for all of us," said Cora.

Dad smiled. "I like that plan."

After an early supper and having changed into pyjamas, they all squeezed on to the sofa together – Mollie May

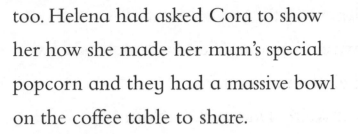

too. Helena had asked Cora to show
her how she made her mum's special
popcorn and they had a massive bowl
on the coffee table to share.

"So, what are we going to watch?" said
Dad, picking up the controller.

"A princess movie," declared Mollie
May. "*Cinderella* or *Sleeping Beauty* or
*Beauty and the Beast*."

Cora's heart sank.

"Not tonight, Molsy," said Helena
quickly.

Mollie May started to pout. "But I
want to watch a princess film! I—"

"Mollie," Helena interrupted. "You've
been a really grown-up girl today,

haven't you? You've done all sorts of grown-up things." Mollie May nodded.

"Well, film night is also a grown-up thing," said Helena. "If you want to be allowed to stay up then you mustn't make a fuss. We're not going to watch a princess film, we're going to choose something that everyone wants to watch. OK?"

To Cora's astonishment, Mollie May slowly nodded. "OK."

Helena turned to Cora. "What would you like to watch, Cora?"

"Um." Cora didn't know what to suggest. What would they all enjoy?

"What did your mum used to like?"

Helena prompted her.

Cora thought for a moment. "Mum's favourite Christmas film was *Elf*," she said.

"Then I think we should watch that," said Helena.

They settled back into the sofa. Dad dimmed the lights and the familiar music started. Soon, everyone was chuckling as they nibbled popcorn and watched the film.

Helena gently nudged Cora. "Thanks for letting us join in with your film evening," she whispered.

"It's *our* film evening now," said Cora. She nestled against her dad and felt a

rush of happiness. They still had a way
to go before they were a proper family,
but she had a feeling they had just taken
their first steps.

# Chapter Ten

"How do I look?" Helena said, standing up and slowly turning round on the day of the wedding.

"Awesome," said Cora, honestly.

"Like a princess!" Mollie May breathed, her eyes as wide as saucers.

Helena had been to the hairdressers

in the morning and her blonde hair was caught up in a loose bun with a few tiny rosebuds pinned into it. She'd done her make-up at home and then Cora and Mollie May, both in their beautiful red bridesmaid dresses, had helped her into her shoes and wedding dress. Helena's wedding gown was made of delicate ivory silk. It was sleeveless and the heart-shaped bodice was encrusted with tiny, sparkling crystals It had a full skirt that flared out from a glittering waistband to the floor. It was elegant and romantic. Helena was wearing pearl earrings that had once belonged to her mother, and a diamond bracelet on her right wrist that

Cora's dad had given her as a wedding gift.

"Can you help me fix my veil?" she asked Cora.

Cora carefully pushed the jewelled comb that the veil was attached to into Helena's hair, just above her bun. The veil was made of pale ivory net and reached all the way to the floor. Cora spread it out at the back.

"There, all done," she said, standing back.

There was a knock on the door. "Hello?" Dad said.

"You can't come in!" Cora exclaimed. "It's bad luck for the groom to see the

bride before the wedding."

"I know. I won't come in but I've got something for you and Mollie May."

Cora went to the door and opened it a crack. Her dad handed her two small jewellery boxes. "The pink one is for Mollie May, the blue one is for you," he said. "They're presents to say thank you for being our bridesmaids. We want you to wear them today."

Dad's eyes softened as he looked at Cora. "You look beautiful, Cora-Flora. I'm so proud of you." He kissed his finger and touched her nose. "I'll see you at the castle."

Cora took the boxes inside and gave

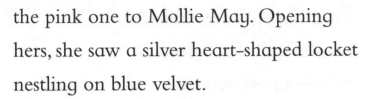

the pink one to Mollie May. Opening hers, she saw a silver heart-shaped locket nestling on blue velvet.

"Open it," said Helena softly.

Cora opened it and saw that inside there was a little photo of her mum, smiling out at her.

"Your dad and I thought that you'd like it," Helena went on. "This way, you can feel like she's with you all the time, not just when you're at the stables."

Cora felt a rush of warmth. "Thank you. I love it." The locket might have come from Dad, but she was pretty sure the idea had been Helena's.

"What's in mine?" Mollie May asked.

"Nothing yet," said Helena. "We thought you could choose."

"I want a photo of you and Joe and Cora for my locket!" said Mollie May, hugging her.

Helena helped the girls put their necklaces on and then they all stood side by side and looked in the mirror. Cora hardly recognised herself in her beautiful red dress and furry white shrug!

"We look like princesses!" declared Mollie May.

"Ready to go?" Helena said, looking at them.

They nodded. Helena took their hands and they headed downstairs.

Annabeth was waiting outside the house with the carriage. The sun was shining in the pale wintery sky, but on the horizon grey clouds were gathering. Duke and Duchess were gleaming white, their harnesses polished and shining. A wreath of flowers and ribbons ran along the back of the seat and there was a white faux-fur rug to keep the passengers warm. Annabeth, sitting in the driver's seat, was dressed in a smart navy coat with brass buttons, a white cravat and a top hat. Alix, who was acting as the footman for the day, was standing beside

the horses in a similar outfit. She pulled
the step down and helped Helena, Cora
and Mollie May into the carriage with a
white-gloved hand.

Some of their neighbours had come
outside to watch.

"Ready to go?" Annabeth asked
Helena.

"Ready," replied the bride with a smile.

The horses set off. Hearing the
clopping hooves, more people came out
to see what was happening. Everyone
waved at them as they clattered past.

"This is so much fun!" said Helena.

Cora became aware that Mollie May
was being unusually quiet. "Are you

OK?" she asked her.

"Everyone's looking at us, Cora,"
Mollie May whispered, cuddling closer
to her and turning her face away from
the watching people.

"Yes, because everyone wants to see
how happy your mum looks – and you,"
she said. She put her arm around the
little girl. "Why don't you wave back to
them?" she encouraged her. "Just like a
princess."

Mollie May waved shyly and the
people they were passing cheered. Mollie
May gave Cora a delighted look and
waved even harder.

Cora felt her heart swell. Maybe it

wasn't going to be so bad having a little sister after all!

They trotted out of town and on to the quieter roads. Soon they spotted the castle on a hill, its stone turrets rising up into the sky. The carriage swept through the grand main gates and as it did so, it started to snow. Large white flakes fell as they trotted up the long driveway, past a lake and through an avenue of tall trees. When they finally arrived outside the huge wooden door, a layer of snow was carpeting the floor. Alix jumped down and helped Helena out of the carriage.

The castle chaplain – the man who was going to conduct the ceremony – was waiting at the doors, dressed in his long robes. "The guests are all in the chapel," he told them, ushering them inside and leading them through the castle.

Outside the entrance to the chapel, Helena took a breath. "This is it then," she said to Cora. She looked nervous but excited. Helena straightened her dress, and Cora made sure the veil was falling perfectly at the back. Then she took Mollie May's hand and they walked through the doors, carrying their bouquets of roses.

The chattering in the chapel hushed as they stepped on to the carpet, and everyone turned to look at them. Cora saw the rest of the Bridesmaids Club waving at her from a pew near the back. She grinned back at her friends and then her eyes fell on her dad. He was waiting at the front, looking handsome in his new wedding suit. When Cora and Mollie May reached him, he smiled, his eyes warm.

"You both look absolutely beautiful," he murmured.

Cora forgot about everyone else and, putting her arms around her dad, hugged him tight.

Everyone in the congregation said "*awwwww*" as he hugged her back and kissed her hair. "I love you," he

murmured. "I'm so happy today, Cora."

She looked up at him with shining eyes. "Me too."

The music changed to the wedding march. Taking Mollie May by the hand again, Cora took her place in the front pew. She turned to watch Helena walking down the aisle, the crystals on her dress glittering and her face wearing a huge smile.

After handing Cora her bouquet of roses, Helena took her place beside Cora's dad. The ceremony passed in a blur. There were hymns, the chaplain spoke about marriage, several people read poems and then Helena and Cora's

dad exchanged rings and said their wedding vows.

"You may kiss the bride!" the chaplain announced.

As Helena and Cora's dad kissed, everyone applauded. Mollie May and Cora cheered loudest of all.

After the ceremony, a photographer took pictures of the happy couple outside the castle, where flakes of snow were falling like confetti.

Cora turned to her friends. "It all went perfectly!" she said.

"It totally did," said Sophie. "Your dad and Helena look over the moon."

"It's so romantic here!" sighed Shanti.

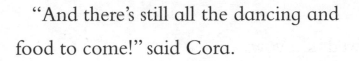

"And there's still all the dancing and food to come!" said Cora.

Emily sighed happily. "I love weddings! I can't wait to be a bridesmaid." She was going to be a bridesmaid at her uncle's wedding in the spring.

Cora looked over at her dad and Helena as they kissed under a stone archway. In their wedding clothes, they looked exactly like a prince and a princess. "It really is a fairytale wedding," she said. "And do you know how it's going to end?"

Her friends looked at her, puzzled. "How?"

Cora grinned at them. "Happily ever

after, of course!"

As the Bridesmaids Club all laughed and hugged, Cora's heart sang. She touched her locket and smiled. She had the feeling that a new chapter of her life was just starting and she was sure it was going to be a good one!

## The End

**Save the date!** Emily's story, **Wedding Day Drama**, is coming soon!

Have you read **Beach Wedding Bliss** yet?
See how Bridesmaids Club began!

Posy Diamond

Bridesmaids Club

Beach Wedding Bliss

Don't miss Shanti's story!
Get ready for a **Big Bollywood Wedding**!

# Bridesmaids Club

*Making wedding dreams come true!*

Beach Wedding Bliss

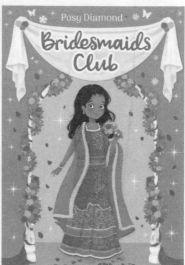

Big Bollywood Wedding

Fairytale Wedding Wish

Wedding Day Drama